OLD LETIVIA
and the
Mountain of Sorrows

NICHOLASA MOHR
Illustrated by RUDY GUTIERREZ

Viking

For Eneid Routté-Gómez and Antonio Martorell,
who welcome me with love to the island of Borinquen where
the spirits of my ancestors sing happily in the chant of *el coquí*.
—N. M.

For Mom and Dad, Elsie Detres Gutierrez and Rudolph Gutierrez.
Mom taught me that royalty emanates from the heart.
Dad taught me that "life is fantastic."
Thank you both.
—R. G.

Author's note: This original folktale was conceived and written when I spent a summer in *el Yunque*, the rain forest of Puerto Rico. While most of the Spanish words are defined in context, *"Lamento borincano"* by Rafael Hernandez is a poignant song that is popular in Puerto Rico, a *bohio* is a cabin with a thatched roof, and *curandera* means healer. Simon is named after Simón Bolívar, the liberator of Latin America.

VIKING
Published by the Penguin Group
Penguin Books USA Inc., 375 Hudson Street, New York, New York 10014, U.S.A.
Penguin Books Ltd, 27 Wrights Lane, London W8 5TZ, England
Penguin Books Australia Ltd, Ringwood, Victoria, Australia
Penguin Books Canada Ltd, 10 Alcorn Avenue, Toronto, Ontario, Canada M4V 3B2
Penguin Books (N.Z.) Ltd, 182-190 Wairau Road, Auckland 10, New Zealand

Penguin Books Ltd, Registered Offices: Harmondsworth, Middlesex, England

First published in 1996 by Viking, a division of Penguin Books USA Inc.

1 3 5 7 9 10 8 6 4 2

Text copyright © Nicholasa Mohr, 1996
Illustrations copyright © Rudy Gutierrez, 1996
All rights reserved

LIBRARY OF CONGRESS CATALOGING-IN-PUBLICATION DATA
Mohr, Nicholasa.
Old Letivia and the Mountain of Sorrows / Nicholasa Mohr ;
illustrated by Rudy Gutierrez   p.   cm.
Summary : To end the devastation of a small Puerto Rican town,
Old Letivia and her friends use her magic to conquer the
evil forces of the Mountain of Sorrows.
ISBN 0-670-84419-5
[1. Fairy Tales.] I. Gutierrez, Rudy, ill. II. Title.
PZ8.M72501 1996 [E]—dc20   95-52188 CIP AC

Manufactured in China
Set in Meridien

At the entrance of *el Yunque*, the rain forest, on the island of Borinquen, lived Old Letivia *la curandera*. Her famous remedies cured colds, fevers, depression, and love trouble. She shared her *bohio* with her friend and companion, a whistling turtle named Cervantes, who was also a clever magician.

Every morning of the week except for the seventh day of rest, they would wander into the dark side of *el Yunque*, where the potent, glistening flora grew. They gathered the wild herbs and plants needed to prepare the teas and potions.

Legend held that mortals who ventured into the dark area of the rain forest were eaten up alive by demons. Not wanting to tempt fate, the townspeople kept away from that secret side of *el Yunque*. They were suspicious by nature, and rumors were rampant. "Old Letivia's a *bruja*, a witch in a woman's disguise," said Doña Hortesia, the town gossip. "I heard that Cervantes was once a mighty king, whom she put under a spell and turned into a turtle!"

"Oh yes," Old Letivia told Cervantes, "they gossip, but they still come out to buy my teas and potions. Why, just last week Amalia Fuentes drank but one cup of my love tea and she married Señor Perez the very next day!"

"We have no need to mix with those townfolks," whistled Cervantes,

who had no use for most human creatures. He preferred to live in harmony with nature, poor but content to accept what fate provided.

A loud commotion sounded one morning as they worked by the river's edge. *"Guaraguao! Guaraguao!"* A cloud of silver feathers swooped down from the tall bamboo trees. The ferocious hawks clawed each other, fighting to get at the floating gourd that was wedged between the rocks in the shallow water.

Old Letivia lit a blazing torch. While the *guaraguaos* screamed in retreat, Cervantes brought the gourd to safety. Inside they found a tiny naked baby who was not much bigger than a ripe chestnut. His face was wet with tears, and his mouth, which was the size of Old Letivia's pinky nail, was wide open. Yet he did not utter one sound.

"Let's see if he can hear, Cervantes." Old Letivia placed the tiny baby in the palm of her hand and rocked him gently, while Cervantes whistled a beautiful rendition of *"Lamento borincano."* The baby stopped crying, smiled the sweetest smile they had ever seen, and touched their hearts forever.

"A greater power has sent us this baby boy, and we must take him home," said Old Letivia.

"He is tiny but valiant. Let's name him Simon," whistled Cervantes. "After our great liberator!"

They took Simon home and showered him with love and care. He was very intelligent and invented his own sign language, which he taught to others. But, as the years passed, little Simon hardly grew. At his tenth birthday, Simon stood no taller than the size of an average coffee pot and had never spoken a sound.

Cervantes and Old Letivia kept a constant watch because scorpions, spiders, and many insects could easily harm Simon. Cervantes built Simon a shield and a spear, a bow and arrows. He became a mighty little warrior, fighting off gangs of rats and large bugs, and battling aggressive birds. Among his best friends were *los coquís*, the tiny frogs that inhabited the island. They played tag and hide-and-go-seek with him and warned of impending danger with their powerful song, *"Coquí, coquí!"* A clan of happy lizards provided him with all his transportation needs.

But no matter how many animal friends he made, Simon wanted very much to play with other children. He began to question: "Why am I not like other children? I am so small and cannot make sounds. Why?" No one could give him an answer.

Old Letivia tried in vain to entice her customers to stay for coconut candy and bark mountain cider. "Let your children stay and play with my Simon." But folks thought all three to be quite odd and shunned her offers. In turn, none of the three was ever invited to other people's homes or asked to be part of public events.

However, within their own little family they were never lonely. Evenings were happy times. After supper Old Letivia would light the fire and make hot cinnamon tea with fresh honey. Then the evening's entertainment would begin.

Cervantes would do magic card tricks, or go inside his shell, levitate, and fly around the cabin while he whistled Simon's favorite tune, "The Flight of the Bumblebee."

Simon enjoyed acting out in sign language how he had narrowly escaped from a gang of mean mice by hiding in Old Letivia's long woolen sock.

Surrounded by the warmth and love in her household, Old Letivia was proud of her little family and had never felt happier. But whenever Simon complained about being different, Old Letivia could not help but worry. "I must pray that one day a miracle may happen, and Simon will grow to a normal size, find his voice, and go to school."

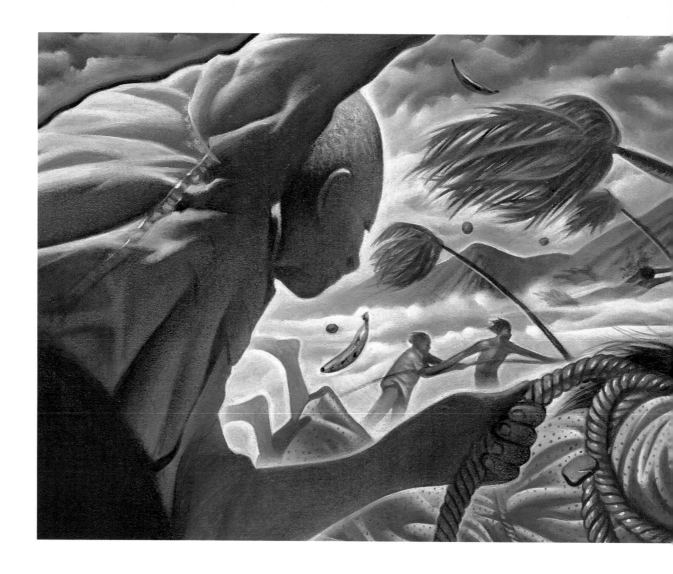

One day a terrible disaster happened. The town was besieged by a horrible screeching wind that lashed out at everything in its path. This Wild Wind caused much damage and devastation. Merchants could not display their goods. Indoors, a blusterous howling rattled through the walls and shook furniture. People fainted with fear. Windows had to be boarded up. Outdoors, vehicles, lampposts, even fences had to be tied down with ropes and cables. Animals were locked in their barns. No one was safe outdoors. People ventured outside only in groups and tied themselves to each other for safety. Time passed and nothing changed. There was hardly any food left. The streets were deserted.

Many town meetings were held, but no one knew how to make the Wild Wind go away. Finally, the mayor made a public announcement.

"We will consult with Old Letivia. Everyone knows that as a *curandera* she has unique powers. She'll save us!"

"No! Never!" protested the Reverendo Duarte. "It is not God's will that we follow the advice of a witch!"

The townspeople argued on. "Well, if she is a witch she must be a good one. Her remedies heal and help us!" Some of them cheered her, while others booed. Finally, there was no one else to turn to. And even those who did not trust Old Letivia decided to seek her out.

Led by the mayor, a large procession bound together by thick ropes marched along the narrow roads and through dense woods until they arrived at Old Letivia's *bohío*. After she heard their plea, Old Letivia recalled the many times when they had scoffed at her offers of friendship. *They need my help, so they are being nice*, she thought. *Well, now it's my turn to be in charge.*

"I must consult on this grave matter with wise friends. If all goes well you shall soon see results. You may all go back to town and wait!" The mayor kissed her hand. Everyone bowed and curtsied before taking leave.

"Hah! Did you see how they groveled at my feet?" snickered Old Letivia. "I'll show them all. After I solve this problem we will be the most important family in town!"

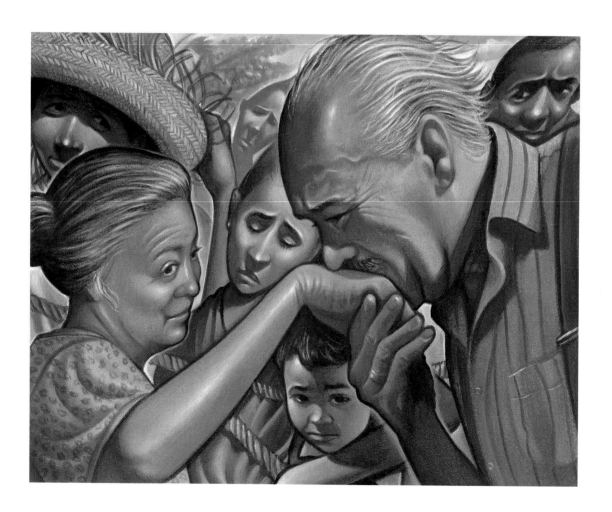

The three went deep into the dark side of *el Yunque* to the most ancient laurel tree, home of Salvador the snail. Salvador was very wise and so old that no one knew his exact age. He leaned out of his large shiny shell and welcomed them. While they sat sipping fresh guava juice, Old Letivia told him her story.

"Let me consult my Sacred Shell." Salvador listened to the ancient shell of his great-grandmother Doña Caracola, the first snail ever to settle in the forest. The shell always revealed the truth and gave wise counsel. "The Sacred Shell tells me that the Wild Wind responsible for this wickedness is hiding up in the big cave at the top of the Mountain of Sorrows."

"Then we must go there, confront this Wild Wind, and make it go away!" cried Old Letivia.

"No! You will face too many dangers!" warned Salvador. "Fernando, the ferocious giant king of toads, guards the mountain. If you manage to get past him you must also pass safely through the Four Peaks of Fear to reach the cave. But even if you succeed to the cave you will be cursed! It is known that all who enter the mountain receive a great sorrow. No one has ever escaped that fate. Take heed," pleaded Salvador. "Nature sent the Wild Wind to the dark side of *el Yunque*. Nature must remove it."

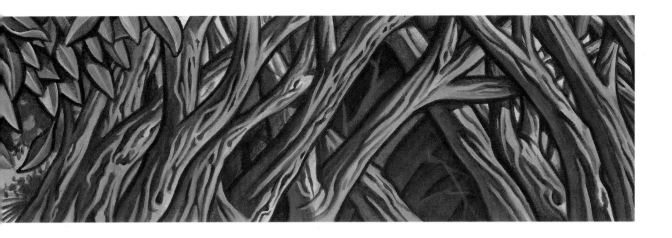

But Old Letivia had made up her mind. "I must prove to the towns-people that I can solve this problem, and become important!" she insisted. "I will not fail. I will bring my magic sack of tricks! We are not afraid, are we?" Simon signaled that he was ready, and Cervantes responded with a solemn, faithful whistle.

Salvador prayed as they departed. "May the good powers above protect this foolish old woman and her innocent companions!"

The following day, before the first roosters began to crow, old Letivia, Cervantes, and Simon had already passed the Lake of Luminous Waters and entered the Valley of Bleakness. The awesome Mountain of Sorrows towered above them, blotting out the heavens. They trembled when they saw Fernando, the giant king of toads, exhaling billows of smoke. He slipped out his tongue and spat arrows of fire at them.

Cervantes spun three times, expanding to the size of a pony. Old Letivia and Simon jumped on his back and soared into the air, leaving the wicked toad in a blaze of rage.

They landed on a gleaming white field of lace flowers. Simon, still perched on Cervantes's back, leaned down to pick one. "Don't be fooled," warned Old Letivia. "These are not real blossoms!"

No sooner had she spoken than all the flowers joined petals, forming an enormous spider web. They were trapped on the First Peak of Fear! Cervantes gave a shrill warning whistle when the huge Spider Monster came crawling toward them. Old Letivia reached into her magic sack and threw a handful of seeds onto the Spider's path, sprinkling them with orchid water. Instantly the seeds swelled into giant breadfruits, barricading the Spider Monster. With a pair of shears she snipped at the web until they were free. While Cervantes flew up to the Second Peak of Fear, all three watched in horror as the Spider Monster devoured the breadfruits.

A wall of fire followed their every movement. Old Letivia frantically searched through her sack and pulled out a jar of hot pepper powder. "Here!" she shouted. "Rub this on your eyes!" A sharp stinging caused all three to sneeze and cry. They cried so many tears that soon they were floating in a pool of water. In no time they swam through the wall of fire and landed on the Third Peak of Fear.

Old Letivia and Simon held on to Cervantes as he stumbled and fell along a narrow road that zigzagged like a roller coaster. Cervantes' shell became stuck on the scaly back of a giant serpent. He could not get free. Old Letivia splashed a thick mixture of bamboo leaf and almond oil under Cervantes' shell. "Hang on!" whistled Cervantes as he rocked and spun

until his shell slid off the scales. In a flash, they flew right up to the fourth and final Peak of Fear.

Blades of grass, as tall as buildings and as sharp as swords, blocked the entrance to the cave. This time Old Letivia took out a rope, tied it around Simon, gave him a pouch containing sparkling sage powder, and lowered him down. "Slip in between the blades," she instructed, and warned him not to touch one single blade. "They will cut like razors." Simon sprinkled the roots of the grass with sage powder, then tugged on the rope, and was hoisted safely onto Cervantes' back. Old Letivia lit a long wick and dropped it onto the powder. Vaporous fumes wilted the blades, exposing a clear entrance to the cave.

Inside the steep dark cave, they pushed their way through slimy spider webs and shooed away a colony of bats. Finally they stood on level ground and stopped to rest. Suddenly, a horrible screeching shook the cave, and a swirl of brilliant colors forming a cloud appeared. It released fire and thunderbolts, narrowly missing them. "We must stand firm and not run away!" cried Old Letivia as all three clung together. When the cloud disappeared it became quiet and dark once again. "Come out, Wild Wind!" challenged Old Letivia. "Stop acting like a coward!"

"Coward? How dare you!" responded a howling voice. "Beware or I will destroy all three of you!"

"Save your threats, Wild Wind," answered Old Letivia. "We have no fear, so you cannot harm us. But we are not your enemies. We only wish to speak with you. Trust us." The colorful cloud reappeared. "Why are you causing so much misery? Why don't you go back to wherever it is you came from?" demanded Old Letivia.

"Because I'm lost. I am a wind messenger from the universe. It's my job to travel and deliver hurricanes, tornadoes, tidal waves, and storms. But I've gone off my course. I have not missed a day's work in one million years!" The Wild Wind began to weep. "My perfect record is ruined."

"Don't cry. We might be able to help you," said Old Letivia. "Tell us how you got trapped."

"When I finished making my storm here I was very tired. I had already delivered several hurricanes and two tidal waves earlier that week. I entered this cave to seek a night's rest. The next morning I couldn't find my way back into the universe. Every path leads me here to this horrible mountain. In order to avoid laziness, I make a storm each day. There's no need to be idle! Then I search for a way out, but so far I've had no luck!"

"It is this evil Mountain of Sorrows that has you under its spell," declared Old Letivia. "But I know a way that will get you out into the universe again." The Wild Wind flew around joyfully. "Before I free you, what can you do for me, Wild Wind?" she asked.

"I can grant you any four things you ask for," replied the Wild Wind. Upon hearing this, Old Letivia was filled with excitement. Secretly she figured that she could save the town, get all she wanted, and be rich, too.

"First you must make Simon like other children and give him speech. Second, you must get us back home safely. Third, you must give me a grand house with a good garden and plenty of livestock. Fourth, everything in town must be put back exactly the way it was before you got here."

"Once I am set free you will have your four wishes. Now, what is your plan, old woman?"

"You will hide yourself inside Cervantes' shell where the Mountain of Sorrows cannot find you. Cervantes will fly up to the summit of this mountain. Once you are safely there, you can leave his shell and go on to freedom!" Cervantes expanded and the Wild Wind spun itself into an arrow, disappearing inside his shell. As they flew out of the cave a bolt of lightning struck Old Letivia and Simon, and they too disappeared in a puff of smoke.

Old Letivia and Simon awoke on a red silk sofa in the parlor of their brand-new home. Both wore elegant clothes, and best of all, Simon was the size of a normal boy. "Mother," shouted Simon, "I can speak and I am like other children." They inspected all their beautiful furniture. Outdoors they found a big garden and a large barn with chickens, goats, pigs, and a milking cow. There was even a grand carriage and a splendid horse. Old Letivia danced, shouting, "I am rich, rich . . . rich!"

As they admired all their new possessions the townspeople arrived, cheering her and asking that she be the new mayor. Everything in town was back to the way it had been, and they declared her a great hero. Old Letivia graciously explained that she did not want to be mayor. She was going to stay home and enjoy her new possessions. "However, now that I am famous you are all welcome to call on me for advice." Everyone applauded and she received many invitations to come to tea.

After preparing an elegant dinner they waited to celebrate with Cervantes. But he never arrived. A week passed, while day and night Old Letivia and Simon patiently continued their vigil. Finally they sought out Salvador the snail. Back at the laurel tree he placed the Sacred Shell before them. An echo filled the air and the story unfolded.

"When Cervantes reached the pinnacle, the mountain trembled and the sky darkened. The Wild Wind tried with all its might but could not leave the turtle's shell. It remained trapped! Tired and weary, Cervantes fell asleep. It was then that the Wild Wind, gathering full force, spun inside the shell and bolted like a rocket—with Cervantes. When they reached the universe and the Wild Wind was back on course, it discarded Cervantes up in the heavens where he landed in the sky. Thenceforth he became a wandering star, destined to travel our solar system forever."

Old Letivia wrung her hands in despair and pleaded for Salvador's help. "No one can help you now," he told her. "I warned you not to enter that evil mountain, old woman! But you would not listen. Now nature has proven who is the more powerful. The mountain has taken Cervantes away forever and has given you a great sorrow. It is at peace. Simon is just like other children; you are rich; the town is safe and happy. You were granted all four wishes and became a great hero." Salvador put away his Sacred Shell. "One cannot get everything and give nothing in return."

With her great sorrow Old Letivia returned to her new life. Simon went to school and had lots of friends. She received many visitors bearing gifts and seeking her good counsel. Yet all of this did not make Old Letivia any less sad. She missed those happy times when Cervantes performed his magic tricks and Simon acted out his adventure stories. The closeness of her little family was no more.

As time passed, everyone worried that Old Letivia would die from missing Cervantes so much. Then one day the townspeople decided to cheer her up by building a statue of Cervantes. The famous sculptor Don Antonio de M. put the statue in the town square for all to admire. When it was unveiled it looked so much like Cervantes that people gasped in amazement. Old Letivia stood tall and happy. "It's almost like having him back!" she sighed.

These days, Old Letivia spends most of her evenings sitting patiently next to the statue. She waits for those wondrous nights when a bright star shoots through the heavens, and a swift beam of light showers the statue of Cervantes with a glowing brilliance. That is when a glorious whistling fills the town square with a medley of Old Letivia's favorite tunes.